Mr Nodd's Ark

Quentin Blake & John Yeoman

ANDERSEN PRESS

This paperback edition first published in 2016 by Andersen Press Ltd.
First published in Great Britain in 1995 by Hamish Hamilton Ltd.
Text copyright © John Yeoman, 1995. Illustrations copyright © Quentin Blake, 1995.
The rights of John Yeoman and Quentin Blake to be identified as the author and illustrator
of this work have been asserted by them in accordance with the Copyright, Designs and Patents Act, 1988.
Printed in China.

1 3 5 7 9 10 8 6 4 2

British Library Cataloguing in Publication Data available.

ISBN 978 1 78344 374 1

Mr Nodd loved doing woodwork. He had a fine set of tools, and he was very proud of them. The trouble was, he was running out of ideas for things to make.

In the past month he'd already made
a wooden umbrella for his wife,
wooden bicycles for his older sons
Ham and Shem,
and a wooden romper-suit for little Japhet.

He still had a lot of wood left. "I know," said Mr
Nodd; "I'll build a boat in the garden!"

"I hope your father knows what he's doing,"
said Mrs Nodd.

With the help of his older sons he built a boat so
enormous that it almost touched the garden walls.

His wife looked out of the bedroom window.
"It's very nice," she said, "but isn't it a bit big?
How are you going to get it out of the garden?"

Mr Nodd hadn't thought of that.

Later, when they sat down to their tea, Mr Nodd was looking very glum.

"You're not knocking the garden wall down," said Mrs Nodd.

"And you mustn't break up the boat," said Ham.

Just then Shem put on the television. The weather-lady was saying that there could be serious floods within the next two days.

"That's it!" cried Mr Nodd, leaping up: "I'll turn it into an ark. And then it can float over the wall."

Ham and Shem thought that this was a marvellous idea.

"I don't know where I'm going to hang my washing," said Mrs Nodd.

"But you can't have an ark without animals. In pairs," said Ham.

"Well, we've got two hamsters and two cats," said Shem, "and two goldfish and two budgies."

"And we could borrow some more," said Ham.

"Very well, then," said Mrs Nodd, "but no stick insects."

The next day the boys went round to their friends and borrowed two rabbits, two grass snakes, two white mice, and two ducks. By a stroke of luck two stray mongrels followed them home.

That evening Mrs Nodd collected up all their wooden cups and plates and cutlery, and the boys got down to making piles of sandwiches.

"We'd better get a move on," said Mr Nodd; "the rain might come quite suddenly. You know, I think we ought to spend the night in the ark."

They all agreed. So they passed the sandwiches and the beds and the guitars, and the bits of pieces that Mrs Nodd had packed, out of the bedroom window and on to the ark.

"Don't you think it's cosy?" said Mr Nodd, lighting the storm lamp.

"Wouldn't it be better with windows?"
asked Mrs Nodd.

"That'd be silly," he replied. "What good are wooden windows?"

They were all just settling down for the evening when they heard a knock at the door.

"I'll see who it is," said Ham.

Imagine their surprise when they saw two large sheep standing there.

"Better let them in," said Mrs Nodd.
"There's still room. Just."

"I wonder how they got to know about it," said Shem.

"You'd be surprised at the gossip that goes on in the supermarket," said his mother.

"Pull the gangplank up and bar the door now, boys," said Mr Nodd. "We could be afloat soon."

The newcomers made themselves comfortable.

"I can't just sit here doing nothing," said Mrs Nodd;
"this could last quite a while."

"Forty days and forty nights usually," said Mr Nodd.

"The weather-lady said until Wednesday," said Shem.

"All the same, I'm getting on with making the
decorations for next Christmas," said Mrs Nodd. "If
anyone wants to help, they're welcome."

Everyone volunteered. The light wasn't very good, and the decorations were rather rough and ready. But they fascinated the animals and kept them quiet.

Finally, tired and contented, they all crept under their hinged blankets and went to sleep.

When at last they woke Mr Nodd said, "We'd better find out what's happening outside. I expect all the house-tops are under water."

"We don't seem to be bobbing up and down," said Mrs Nodd.

"Good workmanship," said Mr Nodd proudly.

"We can't open the door and let the storm in," said Shem.

"I think we're supposed to send a raven out," said Ham. "Would the ducks do?"

"Good idea," said Mr Nodd, and he slipped the ducks out through the cat-flap.

It was drizzling slightly, which pleased the ducks.

They sat on the deck and stretched, and ruffled up their feathers, and preened themselves. Then they spotted a pair of tights caught on a handrail and tugged at them, hoping they were something to eat.

Finally, thinking the others might have got out the sandwiches again, they took the tights back with them through the cat-flap.

"Are the ducks dry?" asked Ham.

"Yes," said Shem. "It must have stopped raining."

"Ducks are always dry," said Mr Nodd. "Rain runs off them like water off a duck's back."

"These are Mrs Next-Door's tights," said Mrs Nodd; "they must have blown off her line."

She held them against her cheek. "Still damp," she said.

"Better give it another day before opening the door, then," said Mr Nodd.

"In that case, let's have some more sandwiches and a bit of a sing-song," said Mrs Nodd.

So they took their guitars and sang, and ate, to their hearts' content. The animals joined in the spirit by bouncing and swaying in time to the music.

They all slept well that night.

The next morning, when they'd woken and stretched, Ham said: "It ought to be a dove this time. Do you think the budgies would do?"

"They're a bit dim," said Shem. "They might forget their way back."

"We'd never get the sheep through the cat-flap," said Mr Nodd.

"And a goldfish is useless," said Mrs Nodd. "Its mind's always on other things."

"Which is it to be, then?" said Mr Nodd.

All the animals looked the other way, as if they didn't understand. None of them wanted to leave while there were still some sandwiches left.

Just then there came a noise like pebbles hitting the side of the ark, and the faint sound of children's voices calling, "Coo-ee!"

"Open up the door, boys," said Mr Nodd. "Those children could be drowning and, crowded though it is, we must let them in."

Ham and Shem flung open the door and looked out. There below, in the sunshine, stood a little group of their schoolfriends.

"We heard the music. Can we come and join your party?" they asked.

The gangway was lowered, and the Nodd family and the animals, all blinking in the light, came out on deck to greet their guests.

"The floods have gone down, then?" said Mr Nodd.

The children looked blank.

Mrs Nodd peered around. "You know," she said, "I don't think we've had much more than a heavy downpour."

Mr Nodd looked very disappointed.

"That's a terrific disco you've built there, Mr Nodd," said one little girl.

"Really?" he said, brightening up. "Oh, thank you."

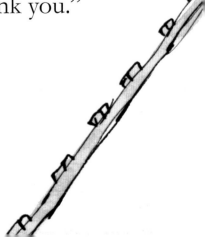

"Now that's an idea, Dad," said Shem. "It could be
ages before the next flood, and mum doesn't want you
to knock the garden wall down…"

"…and you don't want to break the ark up," said Ham.
"So couldn't we use it once a week for dancing?"

"Please, Mr Nodd," they all shouted.

Mrs Nodd looked at her husband. "It does seem a shame to waste it," she said, "and we did have such a good time. Why not give it a try?"

So Mr Nodd got out his toolkit and ran an electric cable from the house so that he could put up coloured lights all round the cabin. Then he set up the boys' sound system and fitted the place out like a real disco.

It was brilliant.

And, do you know, every Saturday evening when Ham and Shem and little Japhet let down the gangway and open the door, there's always a long queue of eager children waiting.

And a few pairs of animals.